4-18-13

To Alexa & Ryan :
Hope you enjoy the book!

Pink is Just A Color
and So is Blue

Niki Bhatia

Niki Bhatia
:)

Copyright © 2012 Niki Bhatia
All rights reserved.

ISBN: 1469902176
ISBN-13: 9781469902173
Library of Congress Control Number: 2012900797
CreateSpace, North Charleston, SC

Look beyond the pink and blues…

what toys are for who..

and focus on the happy children playing and learning!

For my two boys, for being my inspiration.

I love you. NB

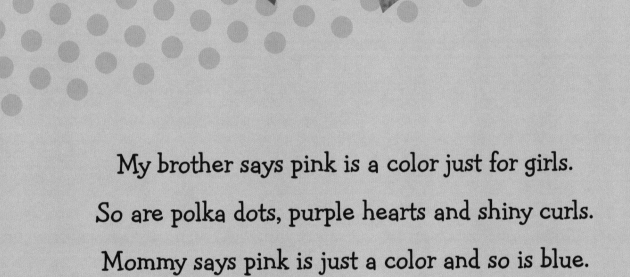

My brother says pink is a color just for girls.

So are polka dots, purple hearts and shiny curls.

Mommy says pink is just a color and so is blue.

Even Daddy likes pink shirts and pink ties too!

My brother says boys don't dress up like princesses

Or wear shiny tiaras… or cute, frilly dresses.

My brother says dolls and kitchens are toys

Made for little girls… and not for little boys!

My brother says I should dress up like a policeman.

Play with dinosaurs... not with aprons and frying pans.

But Mommy says some of the greatest chef are men

Even my daddy likes to cook now and then.

My brother says I should be an astronaut one day.

But I like to sing, and want to learn ballet.

He says I should play soccer, or hockey, or such.

I do like it a little ... but really not too much!

My brother says boys like to tackle and fight

Pretend to be Spiderman, jump from great heights.

But Mommy says boys can be loving and tough.

My brother says boys were made to play rough!

Yesterday I fell and I couldn't help but cry.

My brother said I shouldn't because I'm a guy.

He says boys have to be tough so I shouldn't shed a tear.

Even when I'm scared, I shouldn't show fear.

My best friend is Lily, even though she's a girl.

She likes my dimples… and I like her curls.

My brother says she's a tomboy, but a boy she's not!

She just likes to play with me and the toys I've got.

My brother says Lily should try barrettes in her hair.

Try cute little dresses…which she doesn't like to wear.

She likes playing pirates and crashing race cars too.

My brother says it's *not* what little girls should do!!

My brother says Lily should pretend to be a nurse

Or play with her castle and her shiny, pink purse.

But Lily likes my tool belt....... and power drill too.

Mommy says girls can do... whatever boys can do!

Lily is tough and pretends to karate chop me.

She's a better slugger than any boy could be.

Lily and I like to dig outside for bugs.

I like little ladybugs but she likes slimy slugs.

Mommy says pink is just a color...... like red or blue.

What really matters is what's deep inside of you.

If you looked inside your heart, what would you see?

Just a lot of love flowing through you and me!

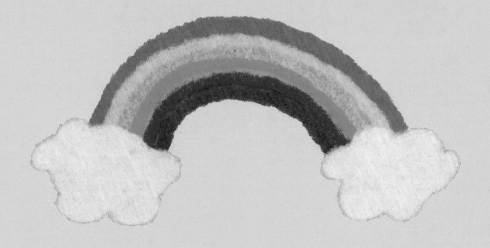

Mommy says that I am her dear, sweet child.

I can be tender and loving, *or* rough and wild.

I can be a fireman or a fashion designer too.

Because pink is *just* a color...and *so* is blue!

Did you know ...?

1. In the 1800's and well into the 1900's, little boys wore dresses up until the age of 5 or 6. Look on the internet for "portraits of Franklin D. Roosevelt as a little boy in 1884" or some of our other presidents as little boys.

2. In the early 1900's, the accepted "norm" was pink for boys and blue for girls. Pink, being derived from red, was considered a strong and masculine color suitable for men. Blue was thought to be cool and delicate, and as such, appropriate for girls.

3. Throughout history, in Europe and in the US, it was fashionable for men to wear curly wigs. Gentlemen also wore shirts with ruffled sleeves and neckline. It was fashionable for men to wear a neck cloth, called a cravat, which was adorned with lace or fringe at the ends. See pictures on internet or in books of George Washington, Thomas Jefferson and some of our other founding fathers.

4. The credit for inventing high heeled shoes is sometimes given to King Louis XIV of France. To appear taller, he had his cobblers make special shoes for him with heels up to 5 or 6 inches high. Other men, and women, also started wearing heeled shoes. He later declared that no one else could wear heels higher than his! Look up pictures of King Louis XIV with his heeled shoes.

5. In ancient Egypt, both men and women outlined their eyes with black kohl. They believed wearing eyeliner would keep evil spirits away. Search for images of Cleopatra and King Tut on the internet.

6. Today, almost 9 out of 10 executive chef are men!

7. Nowadays, more and more dads are staying home to take care of the kids while mommy goes to work!!

Message to parents and teachers:

America is one of a few countries in the world that still believes in gender-specific colors and toys. From birth on, boys are awash in a sea of blue and girls in a field of pink and purple.

From my experience as a mother of two boys, I found that many little boys love pink. They also like playing with dolls and pretending to cook in a kitchen. In fact, when both my boys were young, the play kitchen was the most popular toy during many play dates.

I wanted the illustrations in the book to also send a message. Let's look past all the pink and blues, and what is for girls and what is for boys, and focus on the children. Toys should be just a means of exploring the real world. Allowing children to explore and play freely, gender biases aside, enables them to become happy, secure and confident adults.

The message of Pink is Just a Color and so is Blue is simple. Pink is, in fact, just a color. As history shows, our ideals and ideas change. Today, even old, defined gender roles are changing. What once was, is no more. What is today could be something very different tomorrow. Maybe 50 years from now, our children will talk about a time when blue was for boys, and pink was just for girls. Imagine that!!!

Follow up activity/discussion:

1. Talk about whether the children know of any men (father, grandfathers, uncles, neighbors) who wear pink shirts or ties.

2. Do they know of any men who like to cook?

3. Talk about a time when the men in their lives (father, grandfather, uncles etc.) displayed tenderness and caring towards them or others.

4. Is it true that boys or men should not cry?

5. Do boys always have to be rough and tough? Why or why not?

6. Can or should girls be tough? Give examples.

7. Talk about the activities of the females in the family (mom, sister, grandma, aunts etc) that show that they are able to do many of the things that men do (fixing leaky pipes, painting, mowing lawn etc.)

8. Discuss what a tomboy is and why it's important for girls to be able to do the same things as boys.

9. Look through books and magazines to find men and women in non-traditional roles (i.e. man cooking, man taking care of baby, woman working with tools, woman playing basketball etc.)